NO MORE PLASTIC

by Alma Fullerton

pajamapress

Isley loved waking up
to the sounds of waves lapping
the shore
and seagulls squawking
over the beach:

But early one morning
Isley woke to
different sounds:

CRASHING waves,

SCREECHING birds,

FRANTIC calls for help,

and the distant
  mournful songs
of a right whale pod

vibrating
  across the sea.

Isley ran to help

but they were all
too late.

The beached whale

was
　　already
　　　　dead.

The next day, the headlines read:

WHALE STARVES

DUE TO PLASTIC

FILLING ITS STOMACH

Isley stomped the sand
And kicked at the sea.

She tried to swim away
her anger, hoping
it would float off
with the ocean waves.

But this time swimming
only made her
more upset.

Isley rose from the water
and screamed,

NO MORE PLASTIC

She took a deep breath,
let it out slowly,
and decided to make
a change.

Isley said, "No, thank you,"

to plastic bags and straws
and helped her mom choose
plastic-free products
from the market.

She made a sign
with her grandpa,

and taught her brother
that ice cream tastes better
in cones than in cups.

Isley even wrote a letter
to the mayor
asking her to ban
bottled water.

Everyone agreed
there was too
much plastic
until...

...they all forgot
about the whale
and went back to their old ways.
"Because it's easier," they said.

Isley could never forget.
There were reminders
all around her.

Isley combed the
beach,
gathering up
all the reminders,

day
after
day,
week
after
week,

and

month

after

month...

...until Isley had enough
to build a sculpture
as big as a whale.

Isley's whale
was so big,
it made everyone
STOP
and think big thoughts.

Her neighbors helped
clean up the beaches.

The grocery store
banned plastic bags.

Schools began
zero-waste lunch programs,

and the town installed
filling stations
for water bottles.

Everyone worked
together
for the dream
of a plastic-free world.

Now Isley loves to fall asleep
to the sound of the waves
lapping the shore,

the call of the
nighthawk
gliding over the fields,

and the playful songs
of the right whales:

AUTHOR'S NOTE

Although this story is fiction and takes place on Prince Edward Island, whales are being found washed up on beaches all over the world. Many of those deaths are caused by plastic ingestion or plastic being tangled around the animal. Plastic doesn't break down, so it fills the whale's stomach and they stop feeling hungry, eventually starving to death.

Whales are not the only sea animals affected by plastic in the ocean. Turtles, walruses, dolphins, fish, and seabirds are also washing up on our beaches. Until we find a way to clean the oceans and to stop making new plastic, we will continue to make the ocean unsafe for marine life.

The illustrations in this book were all made using repurposed plastic, sand, and moss.

–Alma Fullerton

Reducing Plastic in our Lives

Here are some steps you can take to reduce your own plastic waste:

- Pack your lunch in lidded containers instead of single-use plastic.

- Use the things you own until they wear out. If you can, fix items instead of replacing them.

- Be prepared! Pack a going-out kit with a reusable water bottle, cutlery, a cloth napkin, and a cloth bag.

Reducing Plastic in our World

A *policy* is a rule or an action plan that a government, school, or business sets for itself.

Like Isley, we can write letters to ask for changes to the policies of the schools we attend, the businesses where we shop, and the towns and countries where we live. If just one business stops using plastic packaging, millions of pieces of plastic waste can be eliminated!

First published in Canada and the United States in 2021

Text and illustration copyright © 2021 Alma Fullerton
This edition copyright © 2021 Pajama Press Inc.
This is a first edition.

10 9 8 7 6 5 4 3 2 1

 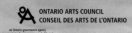

The publisher gratefully acknowledges the support of the Canada Council for the Arts and the Ontario Arts Council for its publishing program. We acknowledge the financial support of the Government of Canada through the Canada Book Fund (CBF) for our publishing activities.

Library and Archives Canada Cataloguing in Publication
Title: No more plastic / by Alma Fullerton.
Names: Fullerton, Alma, author, illustrator.
Identifiers: Canadiana 20200374036 | ISBN 9781772781137 (hardcover)
Classification: LCC PS8611.U45 N6 2021 | DDC jC813/.6—dc23

Publisher Cataloging-in-Publication Data (U.S.)
Names: Fullerton, Alma, author, illustrator.
Title: No More Plastic / by Alma Fullerton.
Description: Toronto, Ontario Canada : Pajama Press, 2021. | Summary: "When she sees a beached whale that has starved to death after ingesting plastic, a young girl named Isley is inspired to adopt a plastic-free lifestyle, encouraging her family to join her. When people start falling back into old habits, Isley builds a plastic sculpture of a whale that inspires lasting change"– Provided by publisher.
Identifiers: ISBN 978-1-77278-113-7 (hardback)
Subjects: LCSH: Children and the environment -- Juvenile fiction. | Plastic scrap -- Juvenile fiction. | Recycling (Waste, etc.) in art -- Juvenile fiction. | BISAC: JUVENILE FICTION / Recycling & Green Living. | JUVENILE FICTION / Science & Nature / Environment. | JUVENILE FICTION / Animals / Marine Life.
Classification: LCC PZ7.F855No |DDC [F] – dc23

Cover and book design—Rebecca Bender and Lorena González Guillén

Printed in China by WKT Company

Pajama Press Inc.
469 Richmond St. E, Toronto, Ontario, Canada, M5A 1R1

Distributed in Canada by UTP Distribution
5201 Dufferin Street Toronto, Ontario Canada, M3H 5T8

Distributed in the U.S. by Ingram Publisher Services
1 Ingram Blvd. La Vergne, TN 37086, USA

Original diorama art created
with found plastic waste, acrylic
paint, sand, and digital

Dedicated to Annabelle, Jacob, and every child who does little things to make big changes in our world

—A.F.